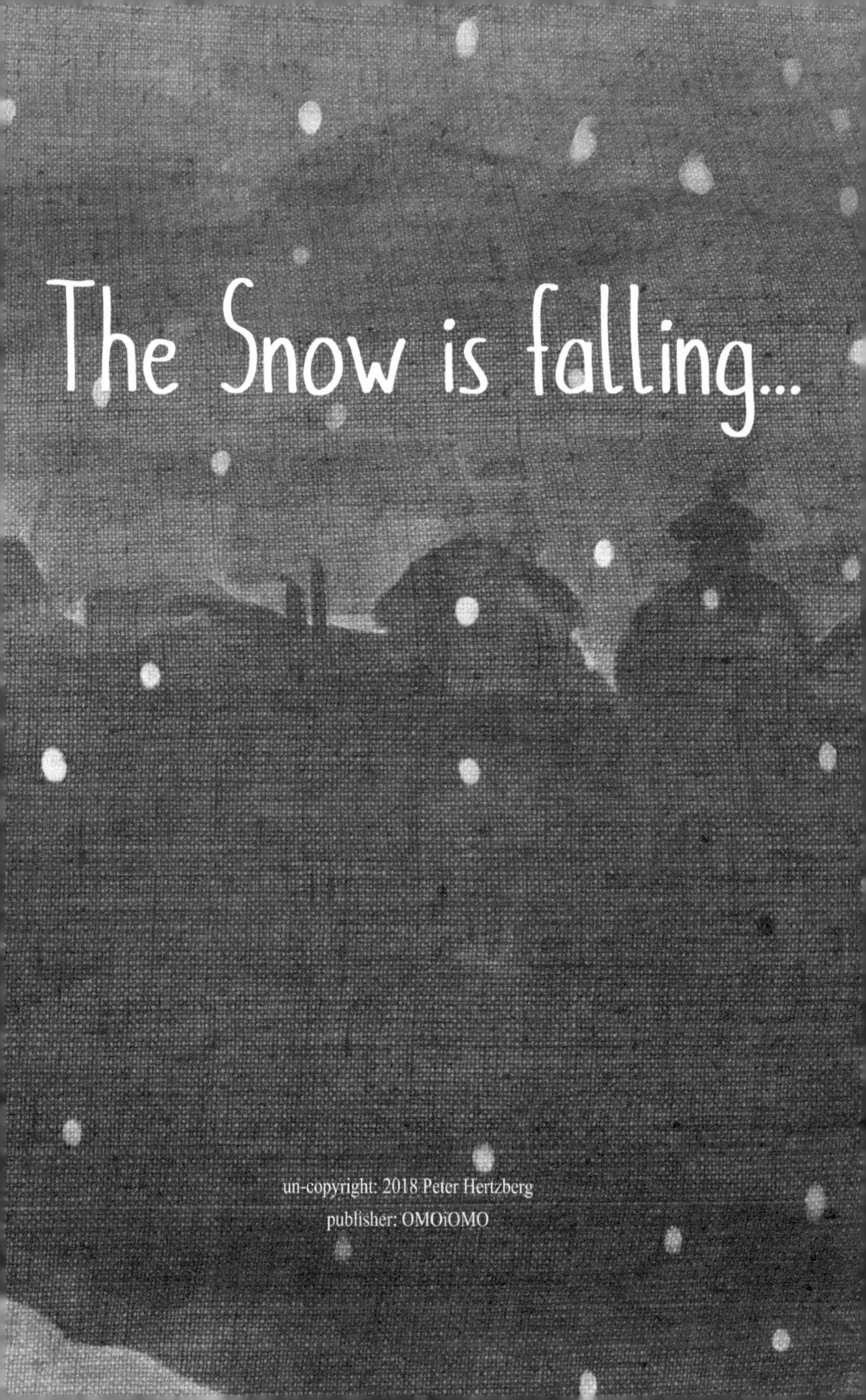

The Snow is falling...

publisher: OMOiOMO

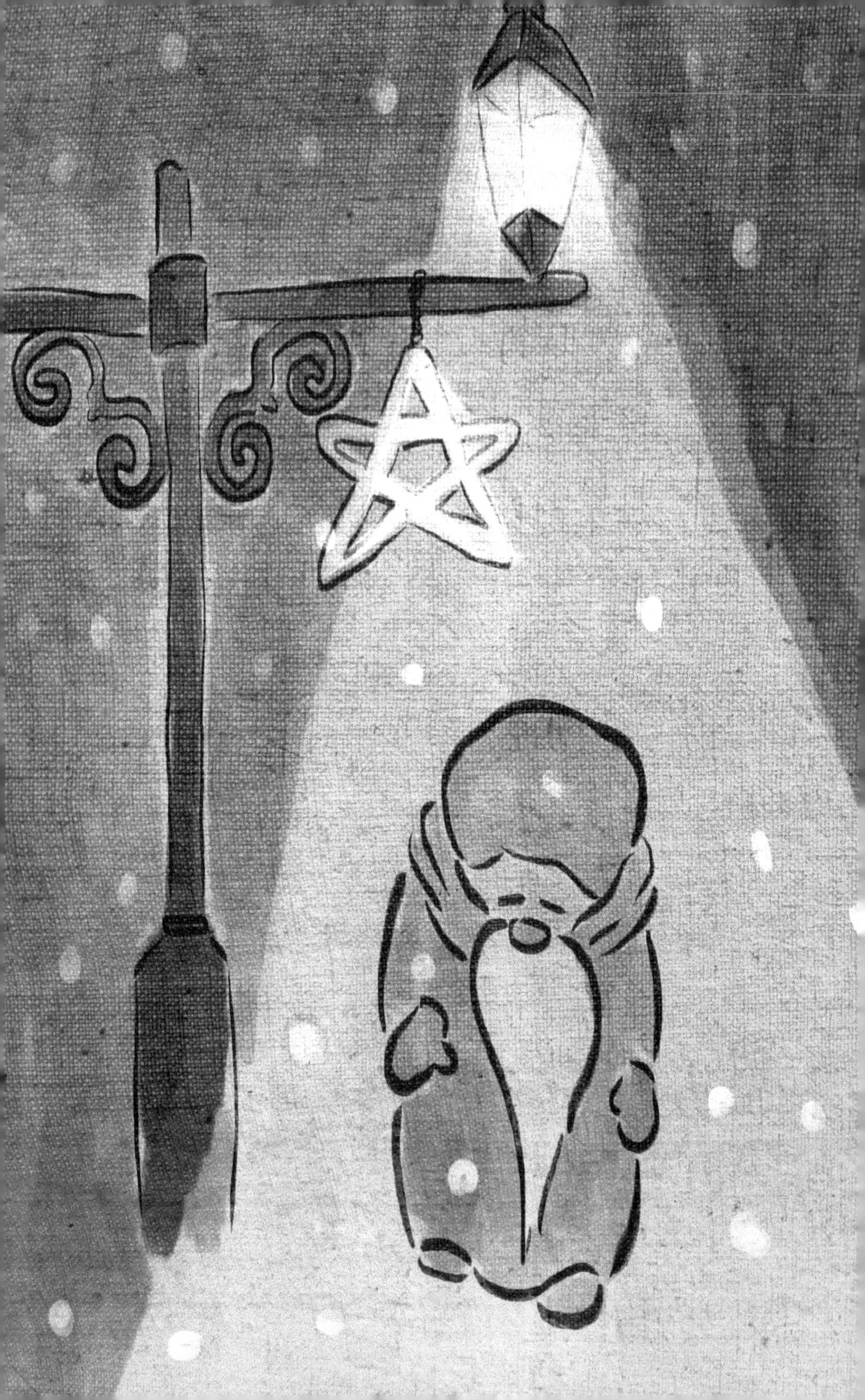

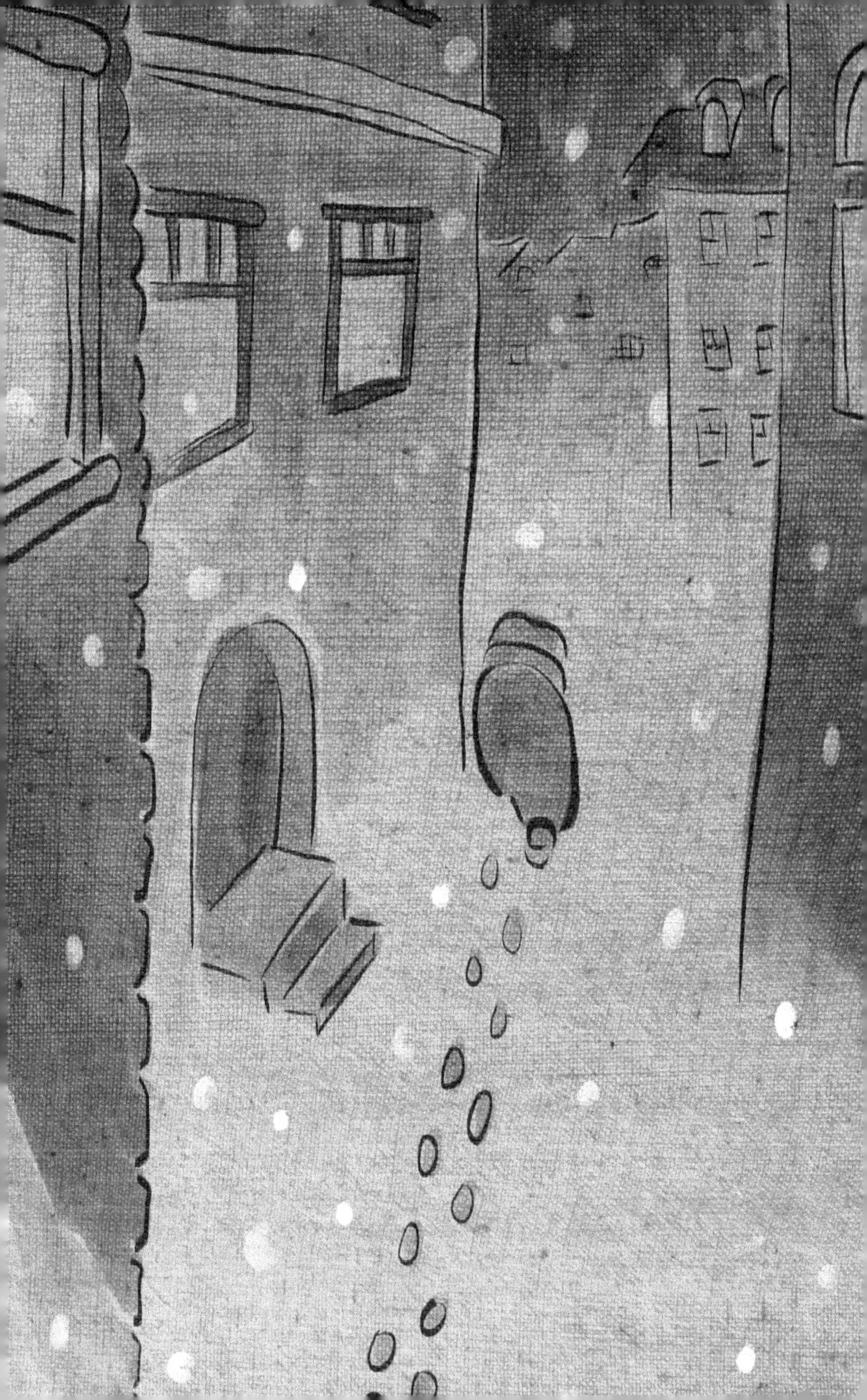

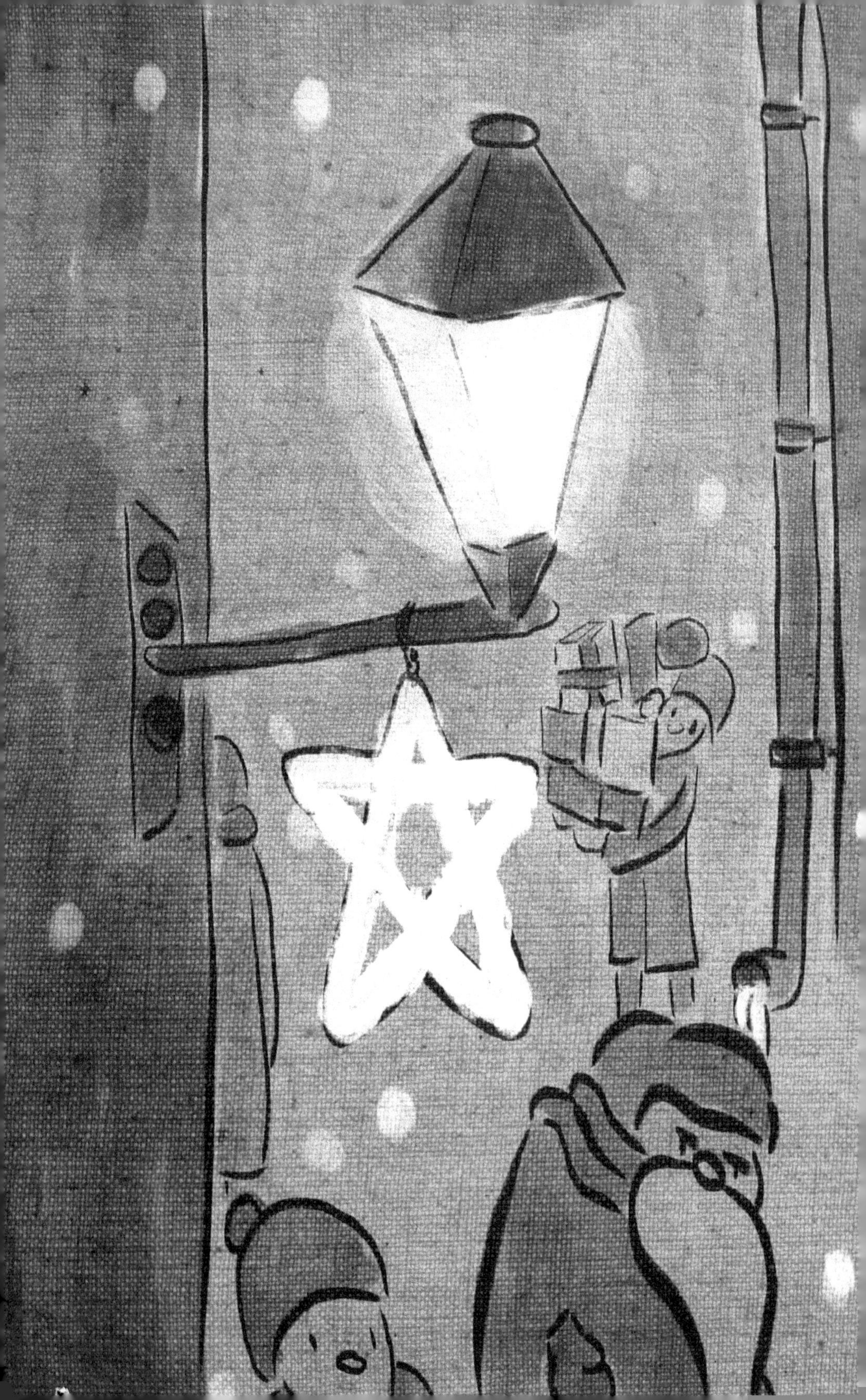

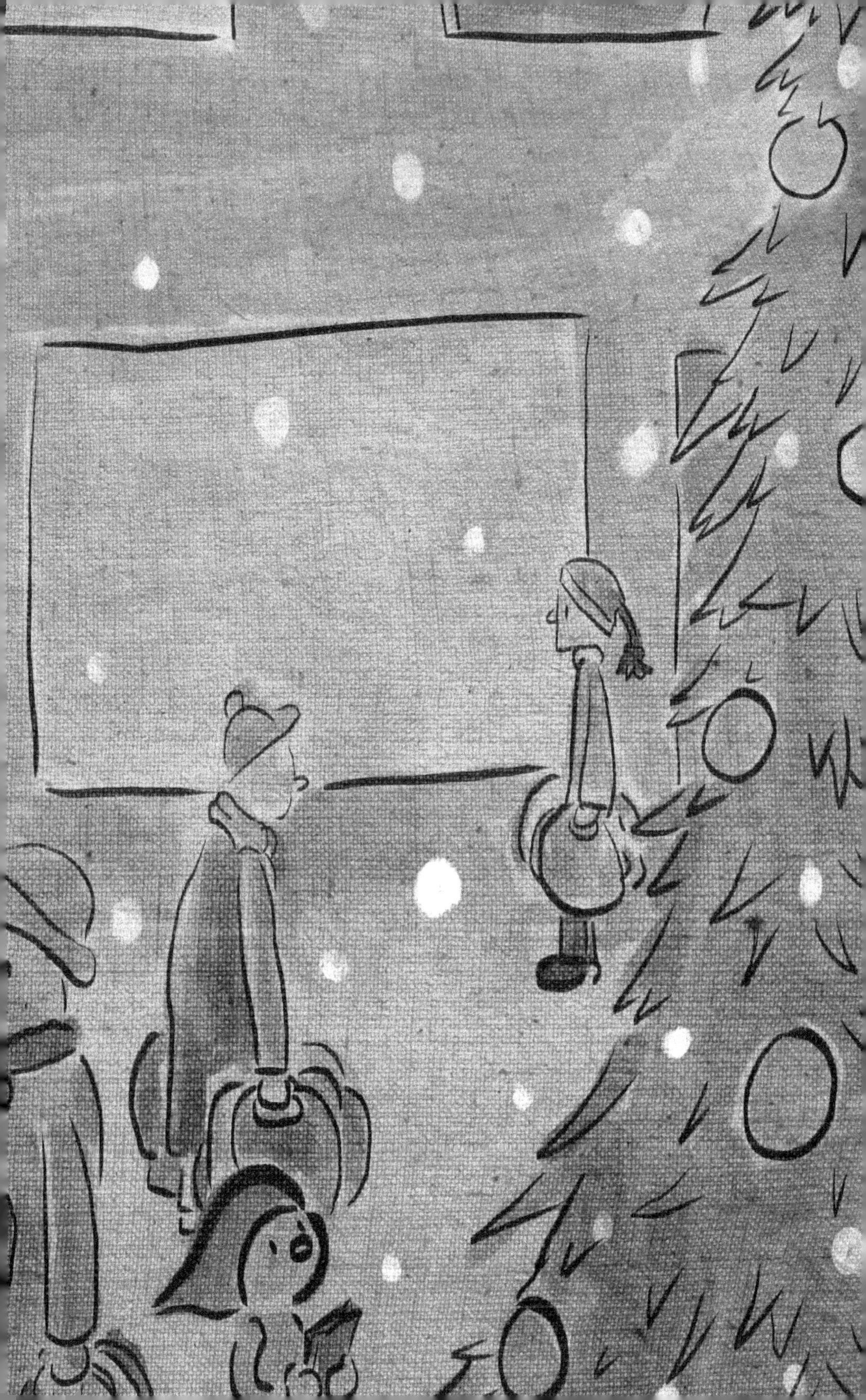

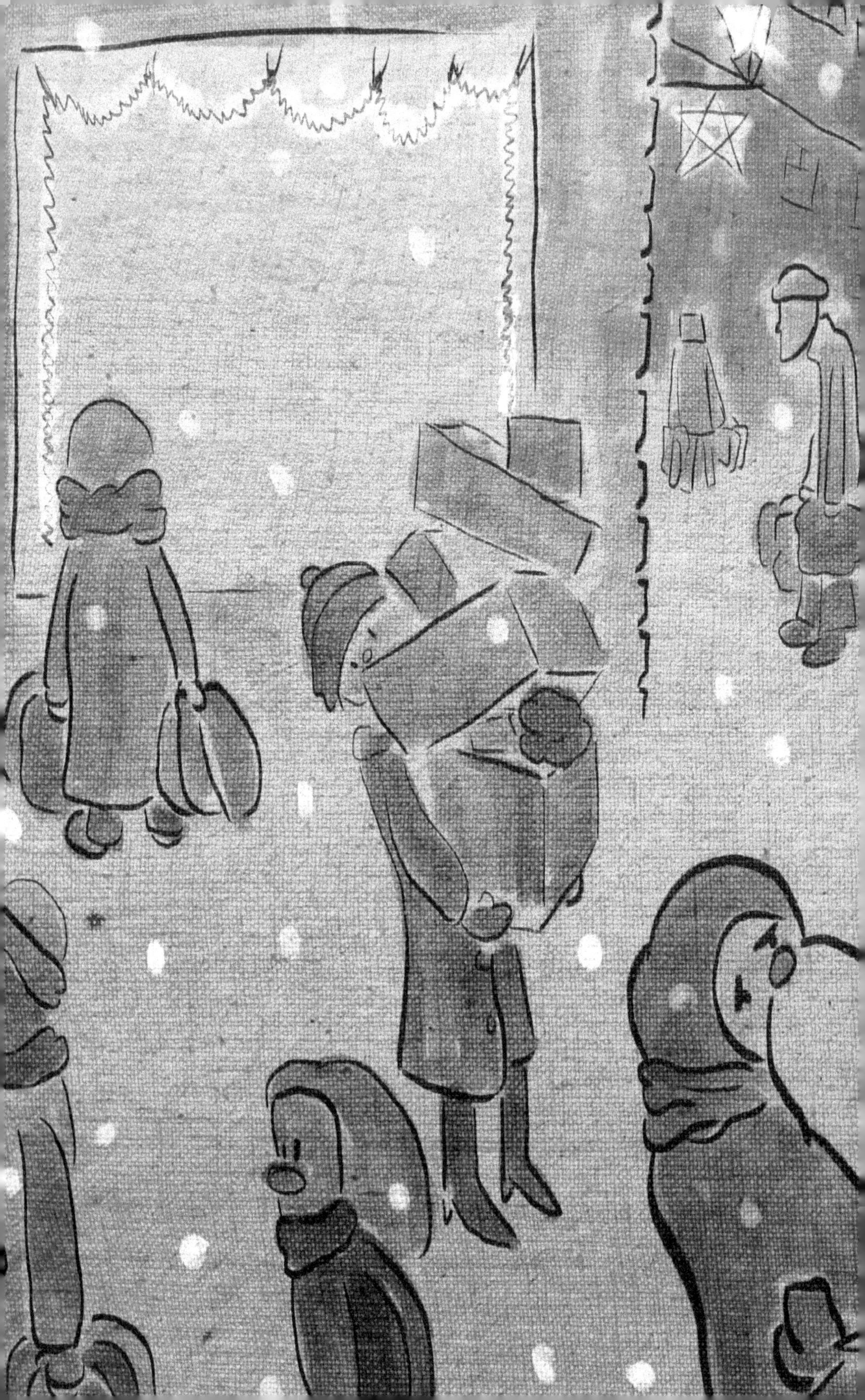

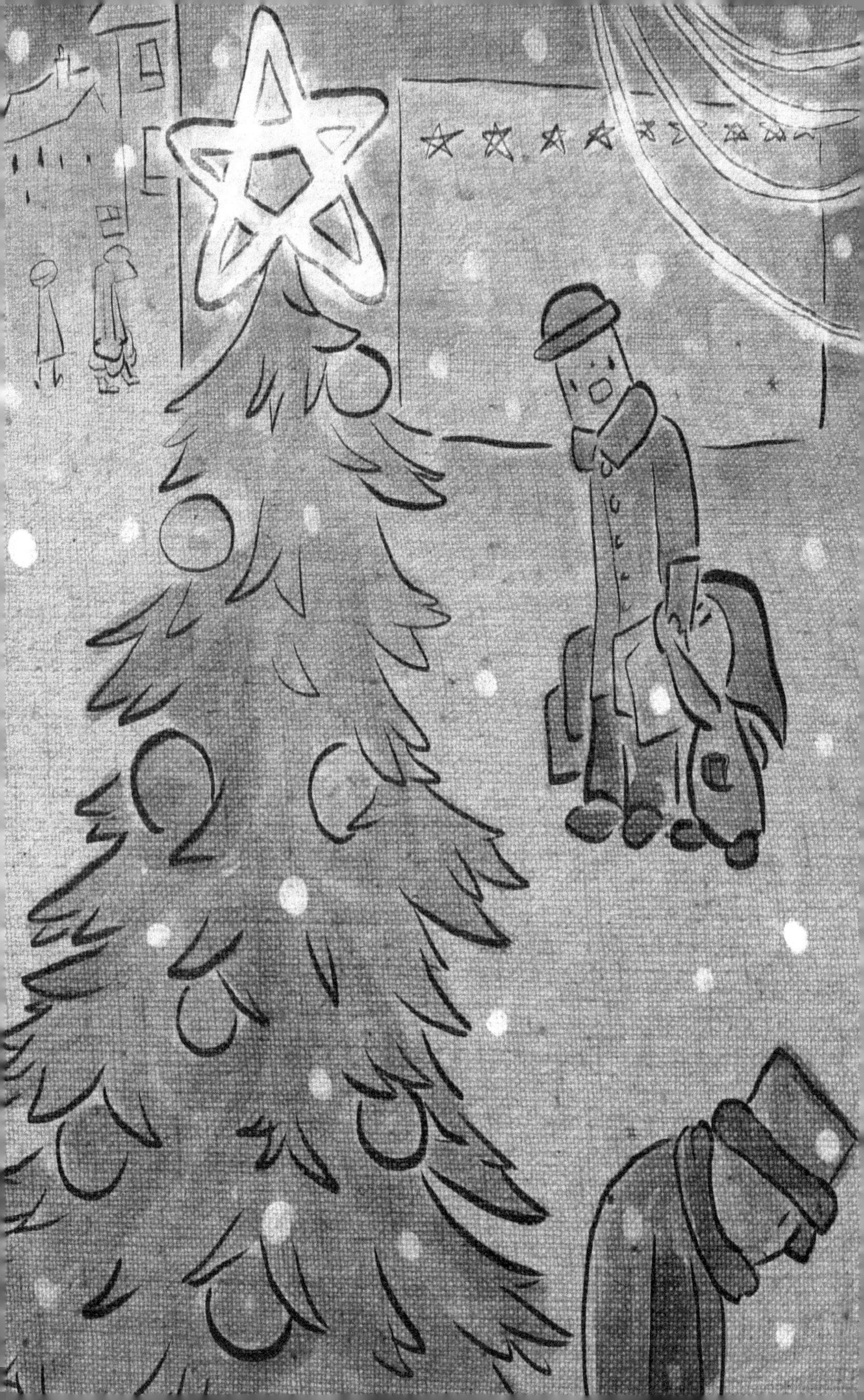

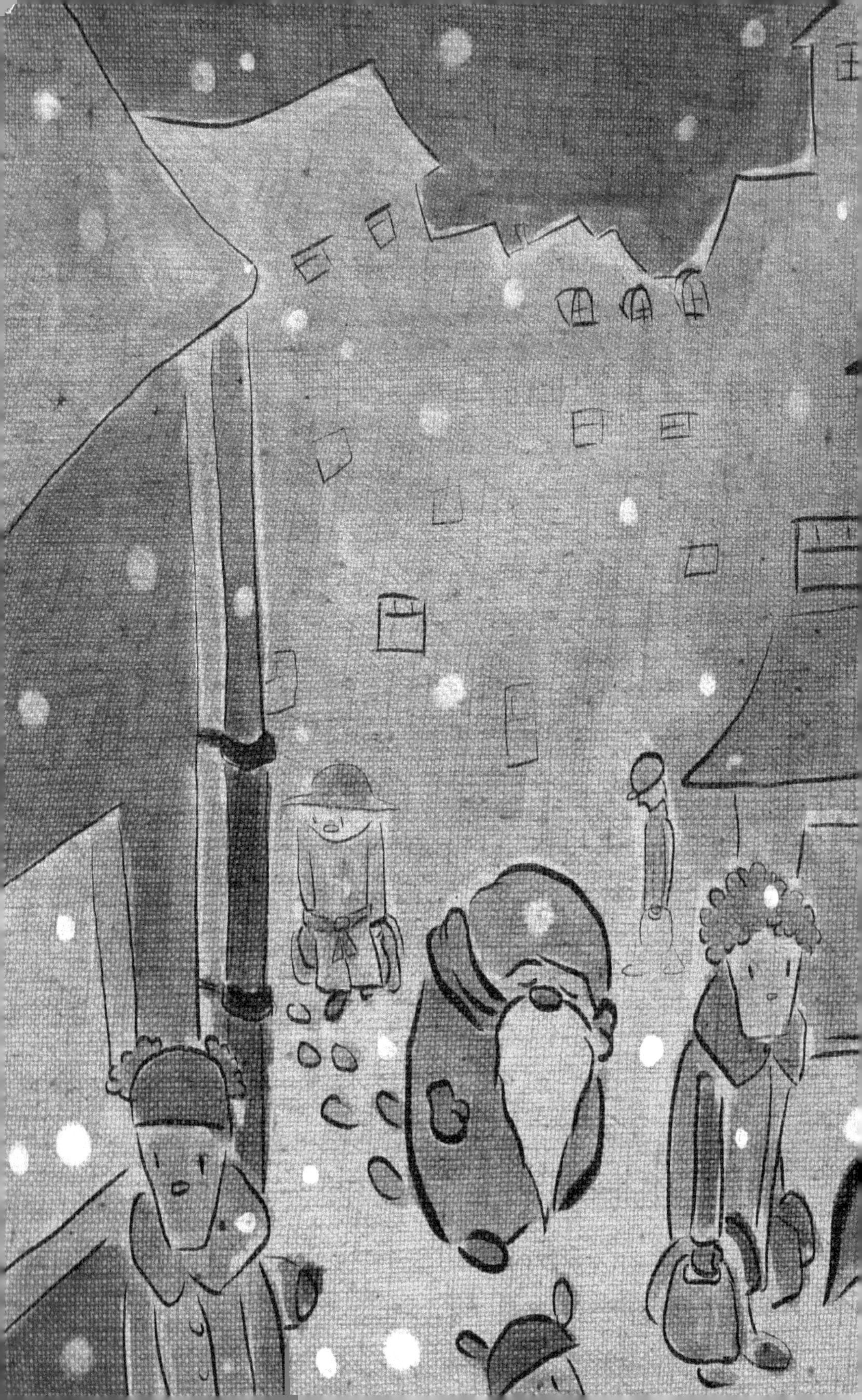

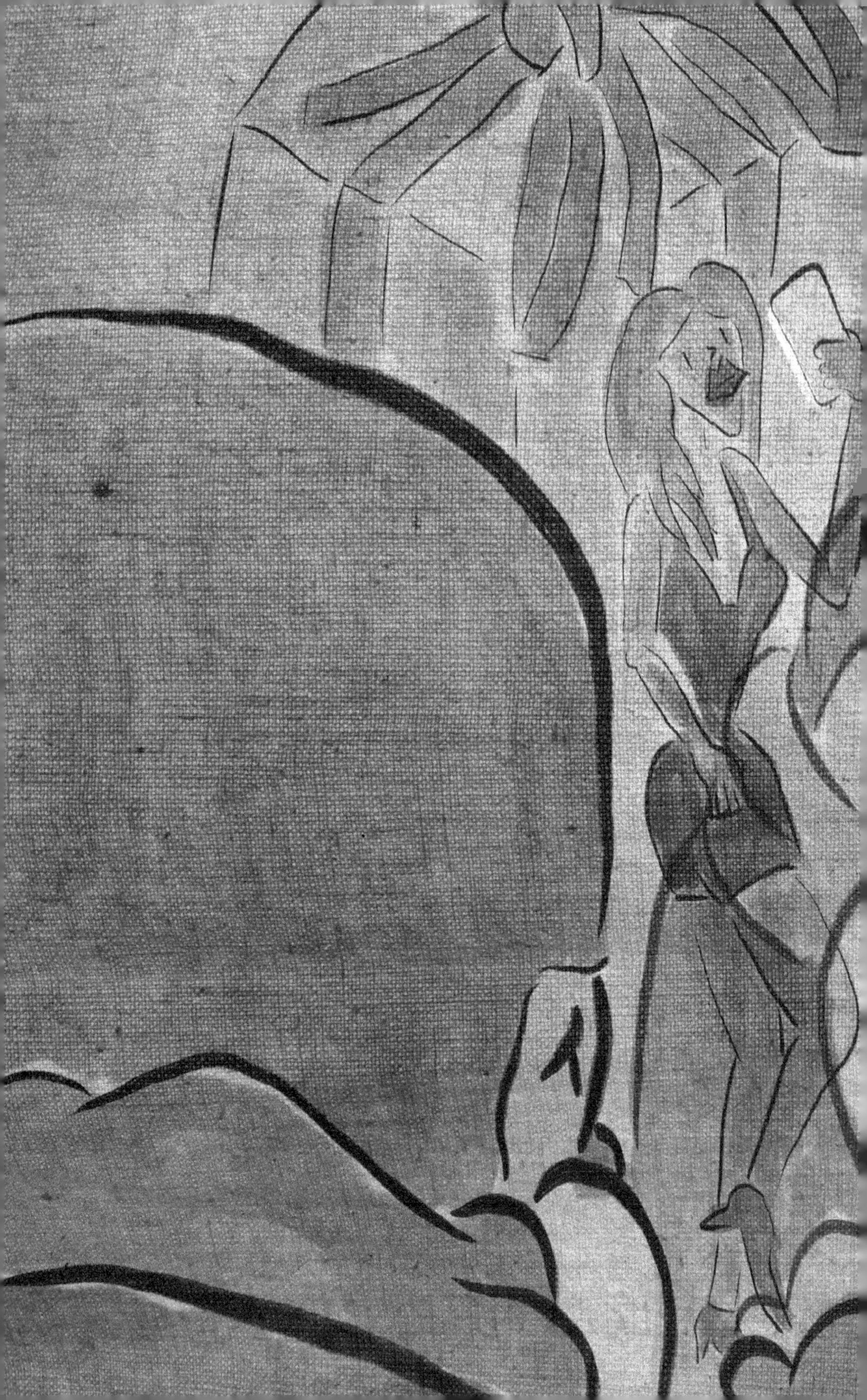

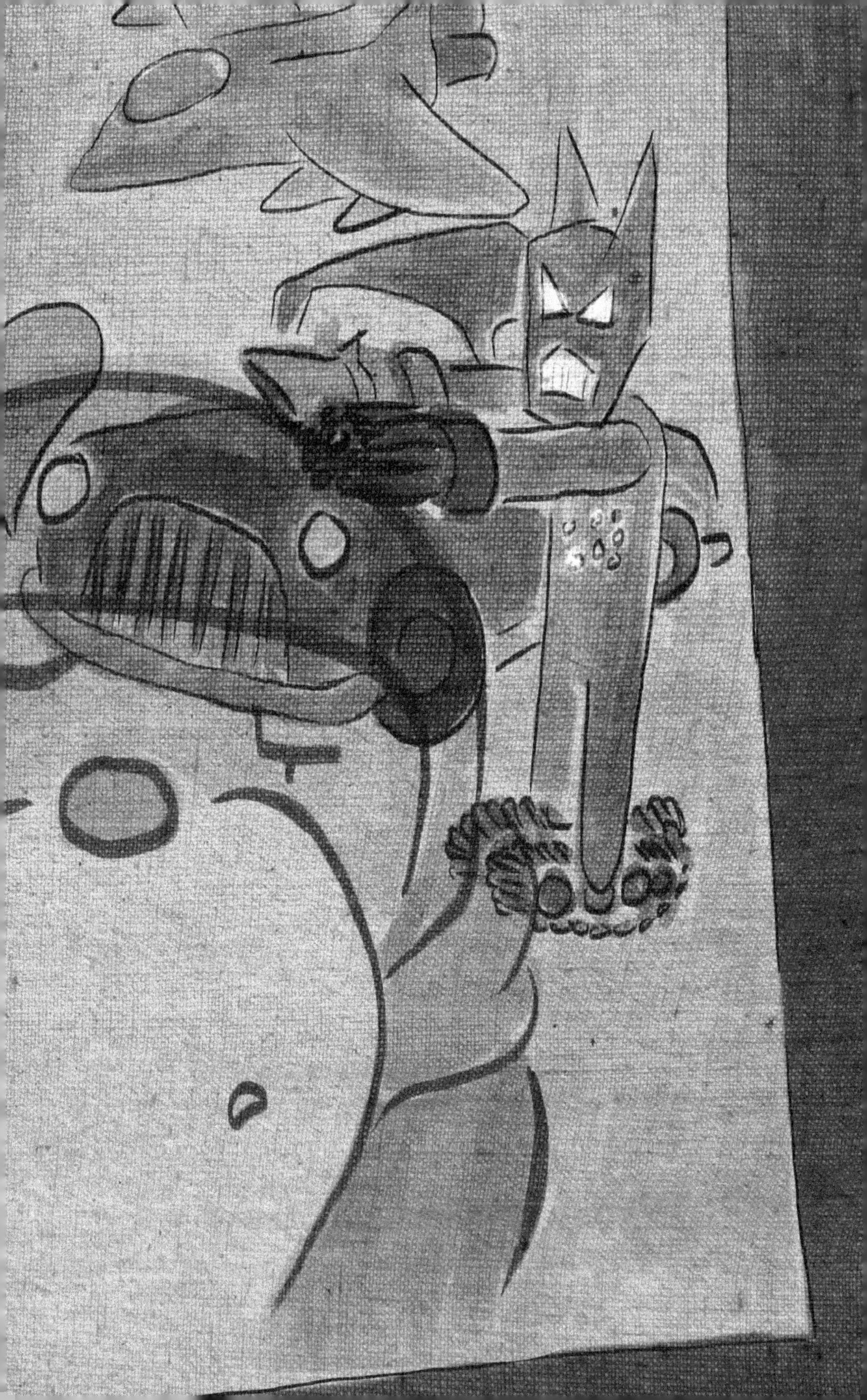

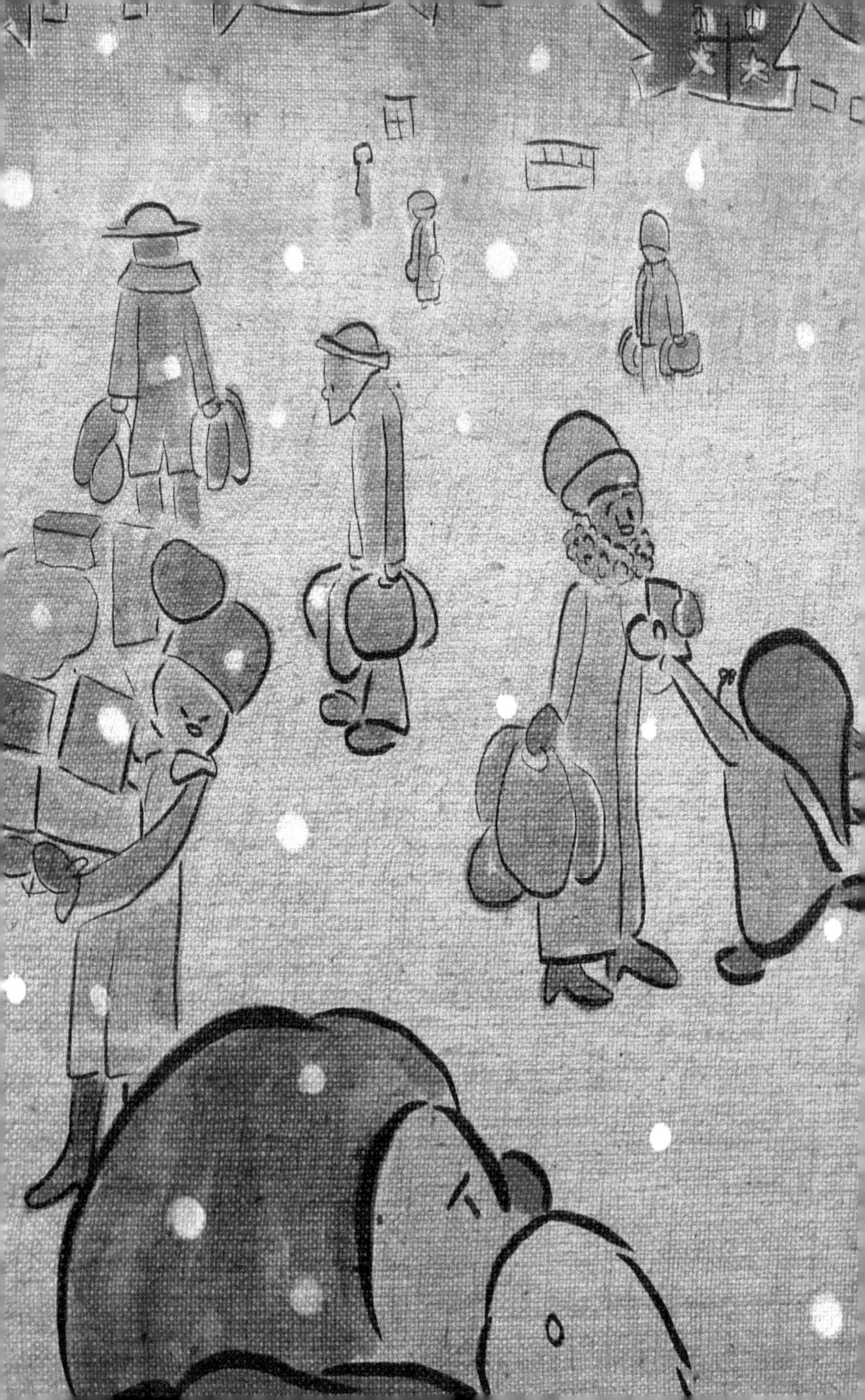

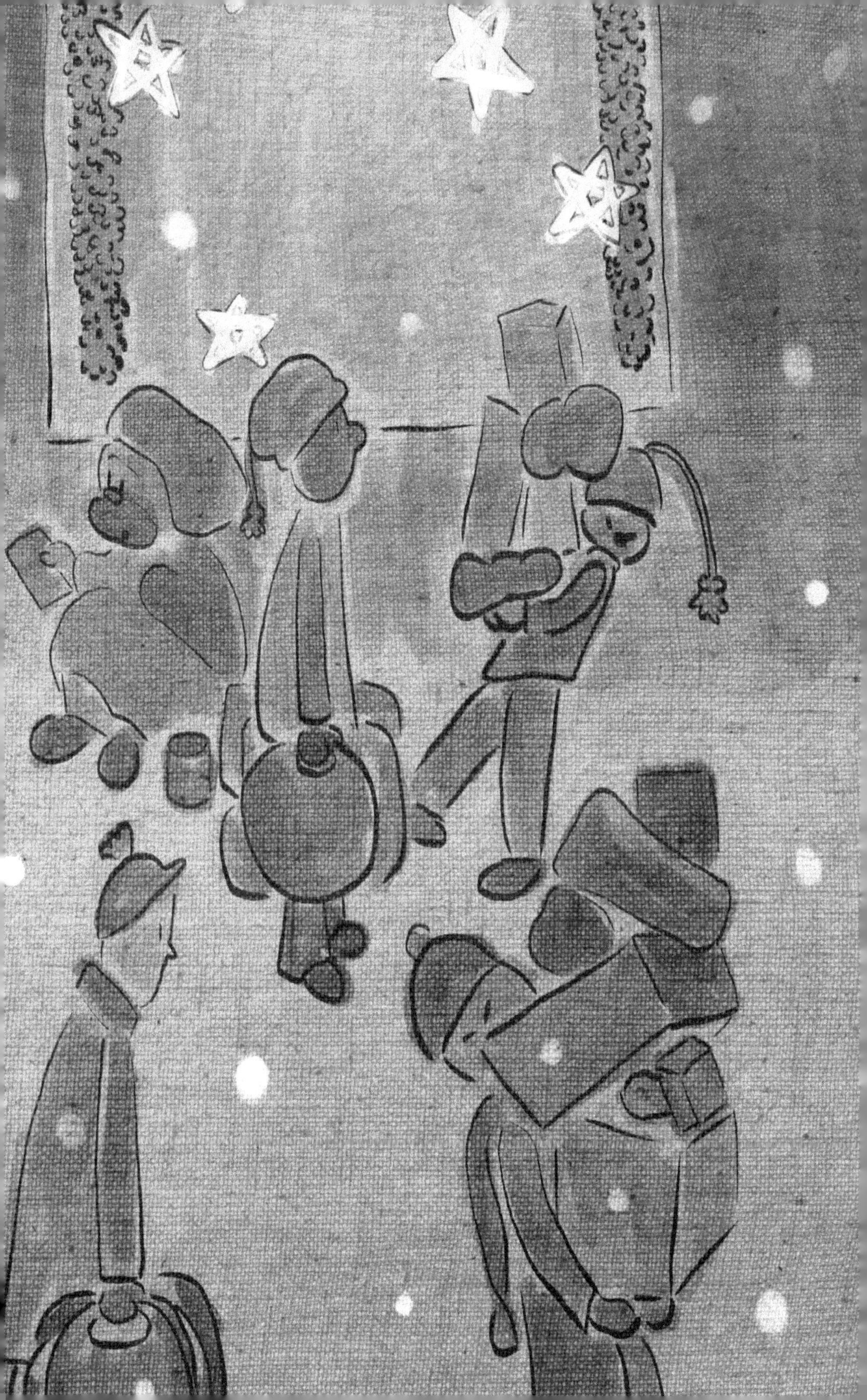

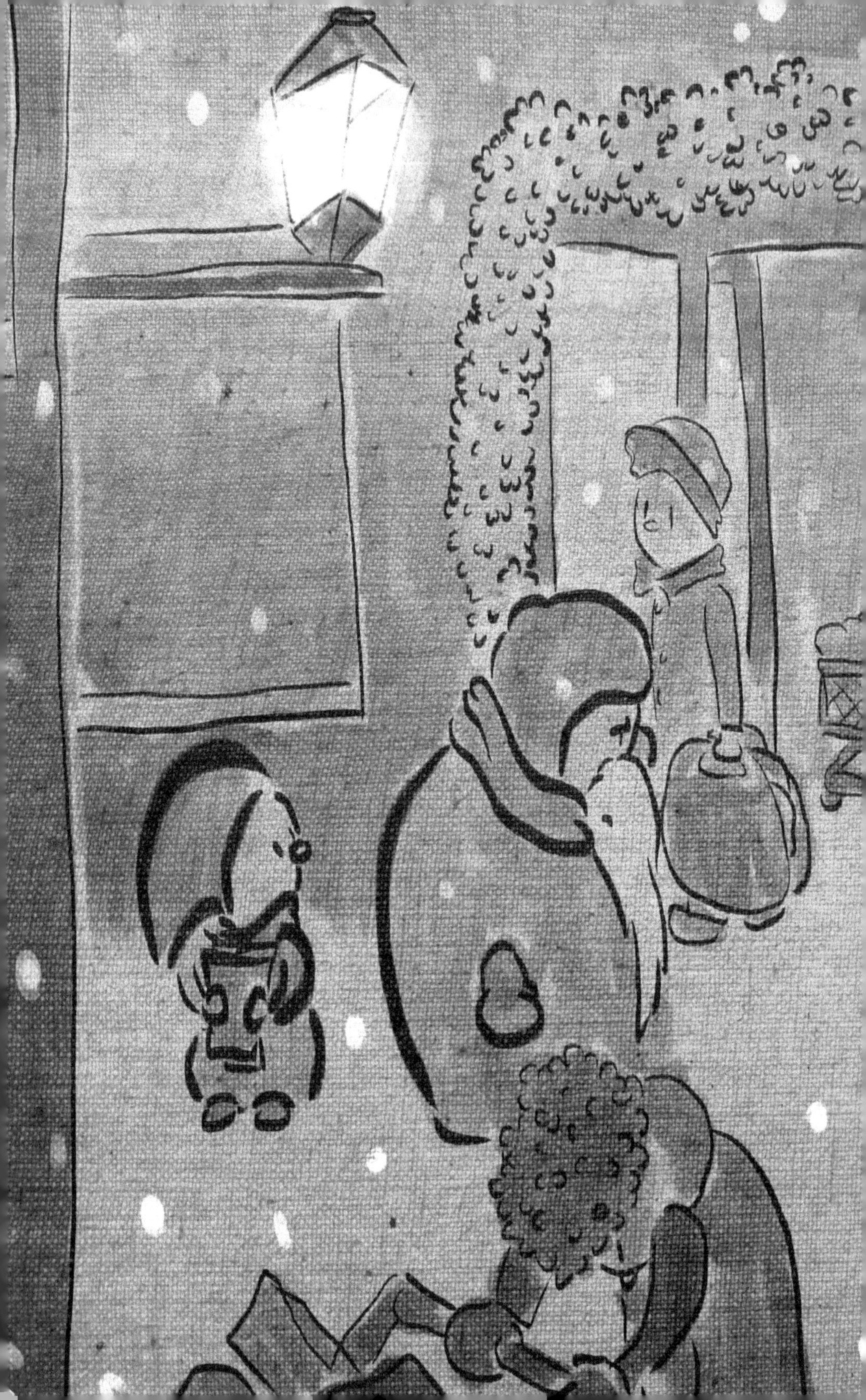

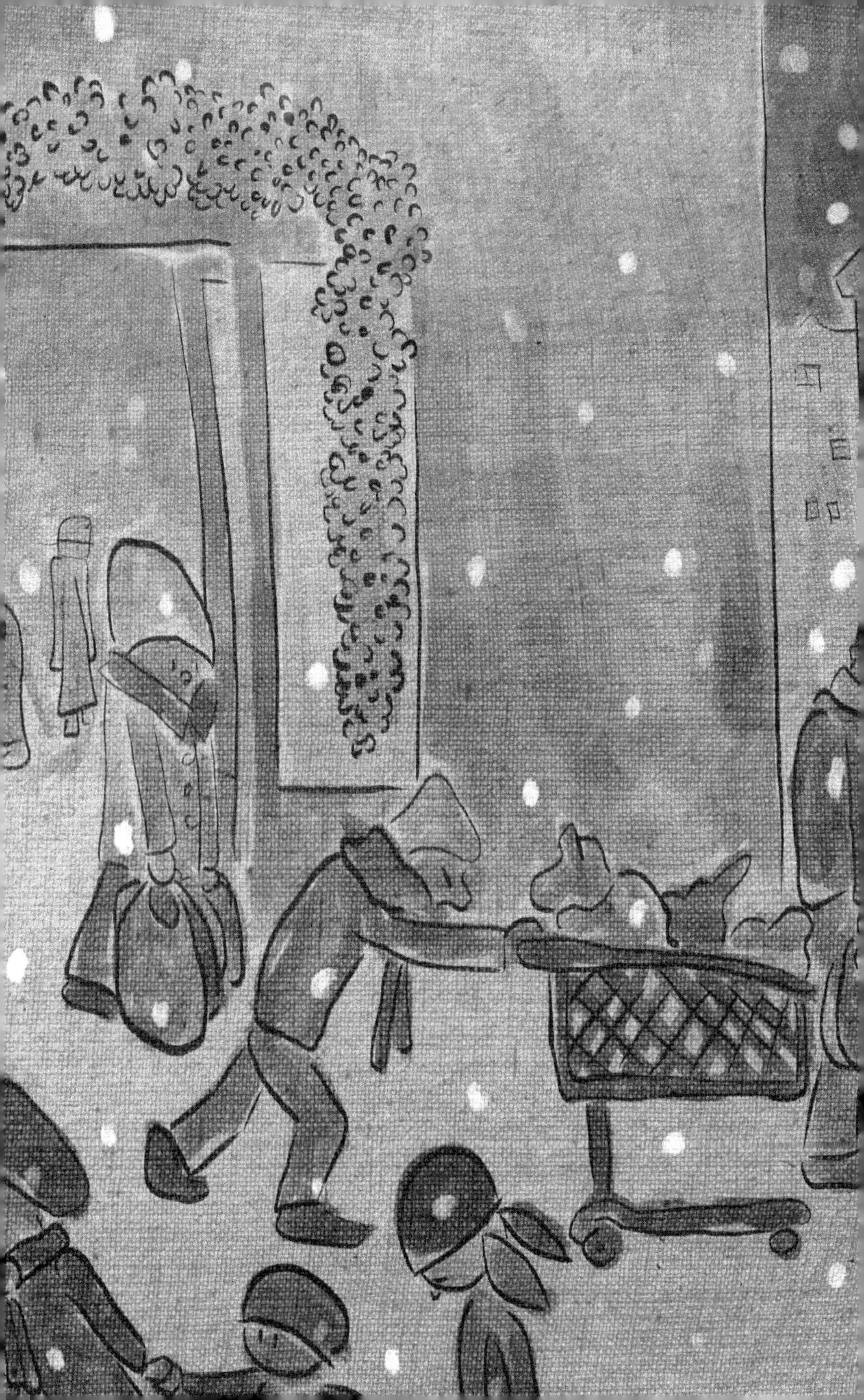

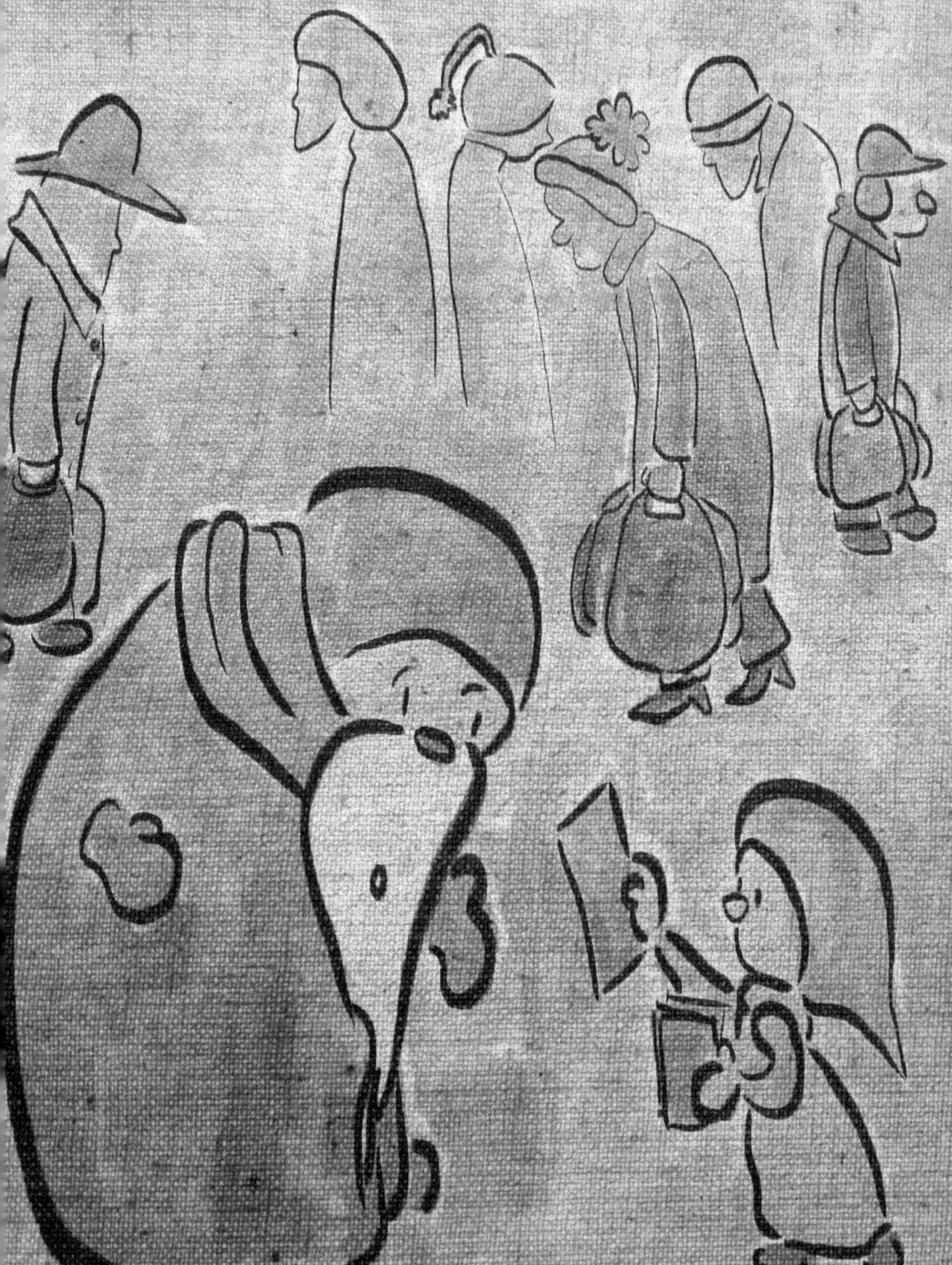

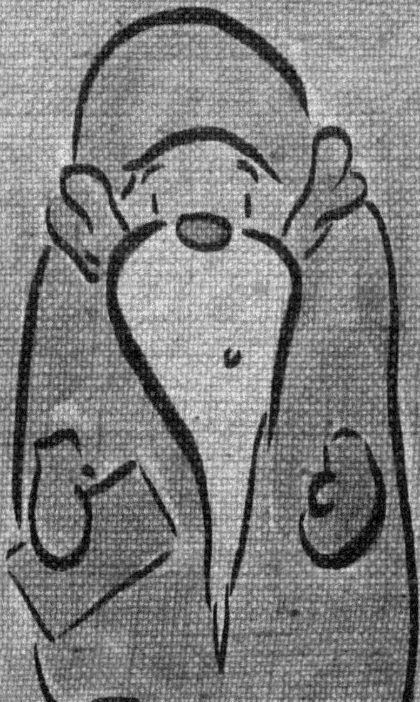

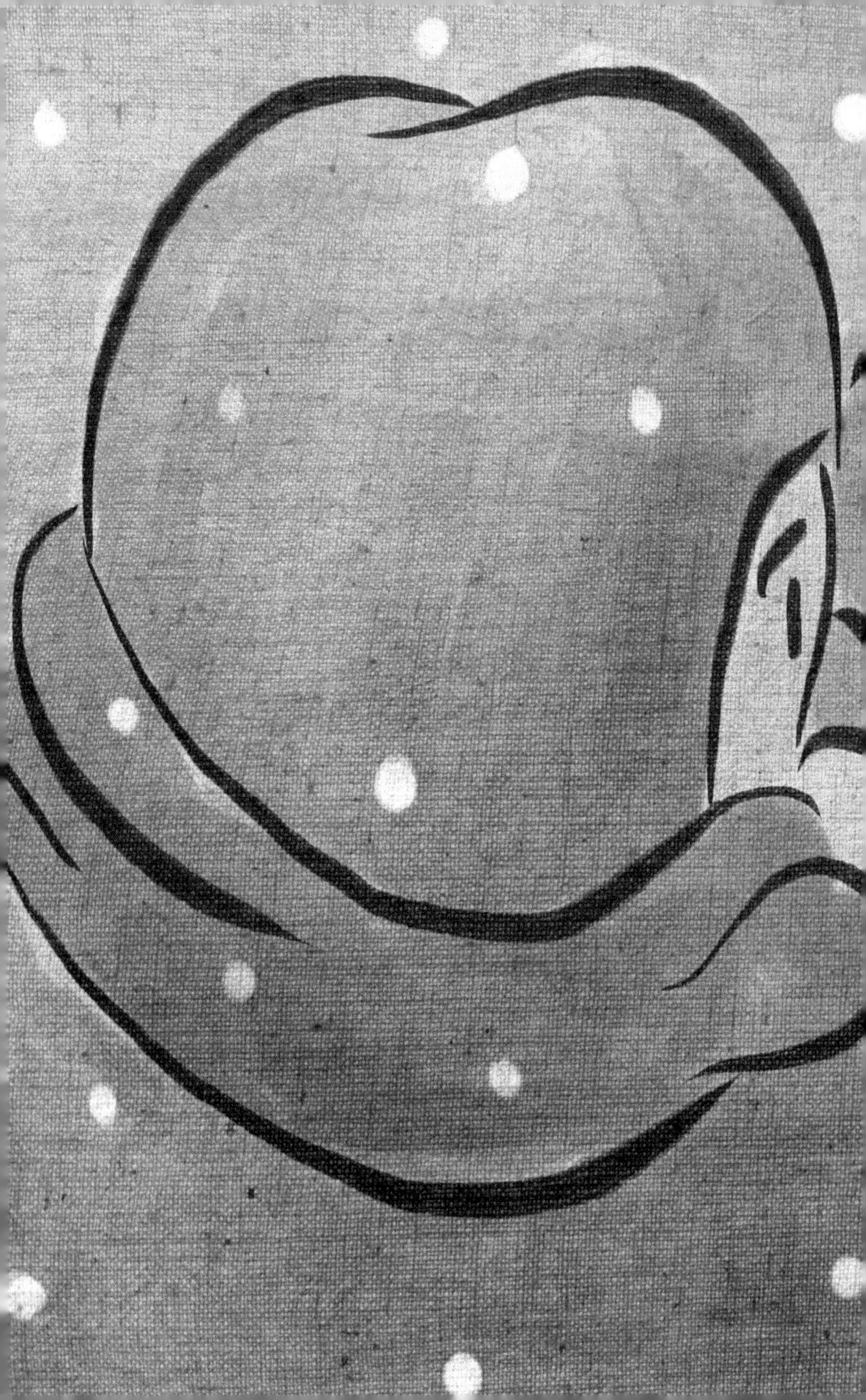

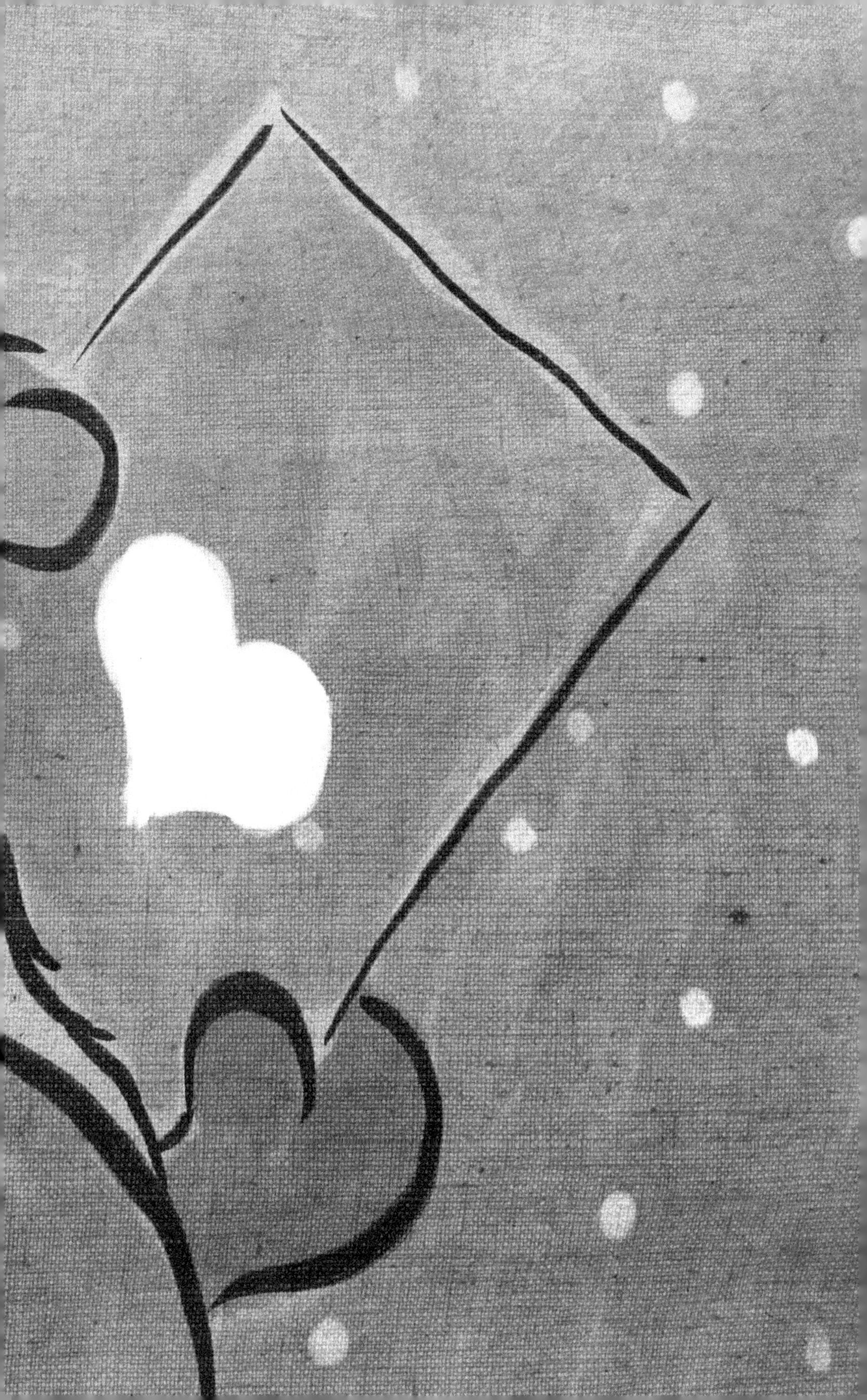

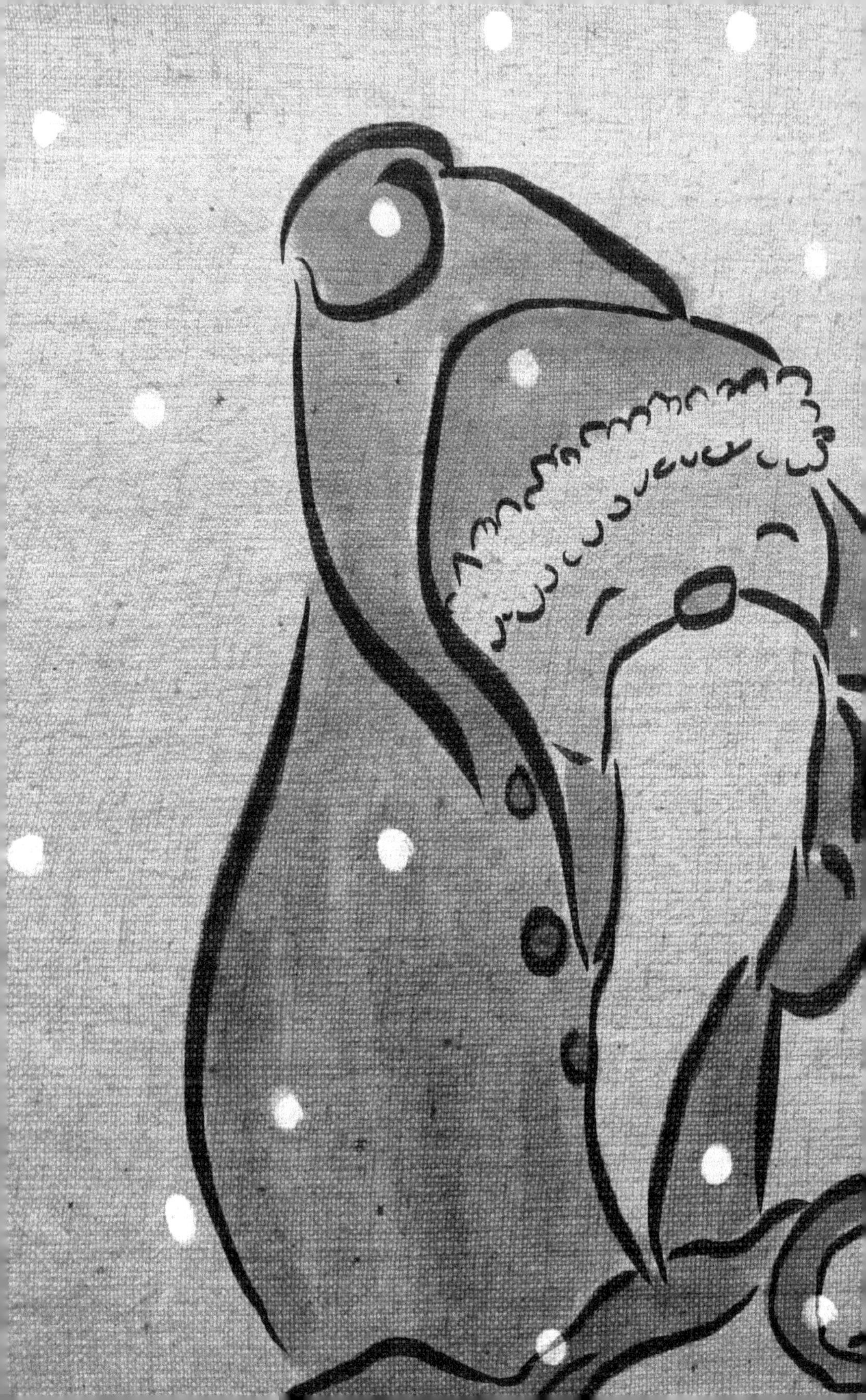

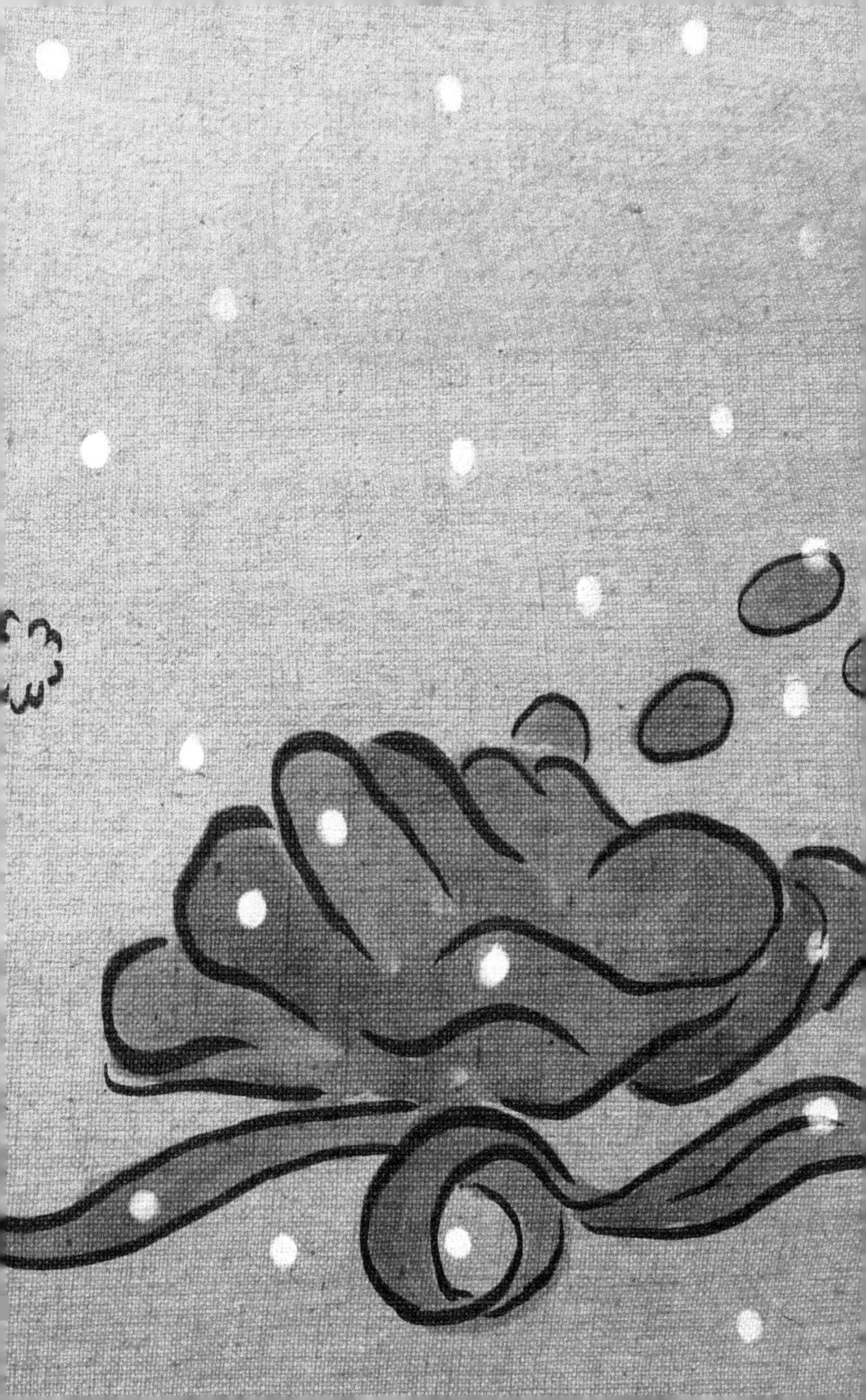

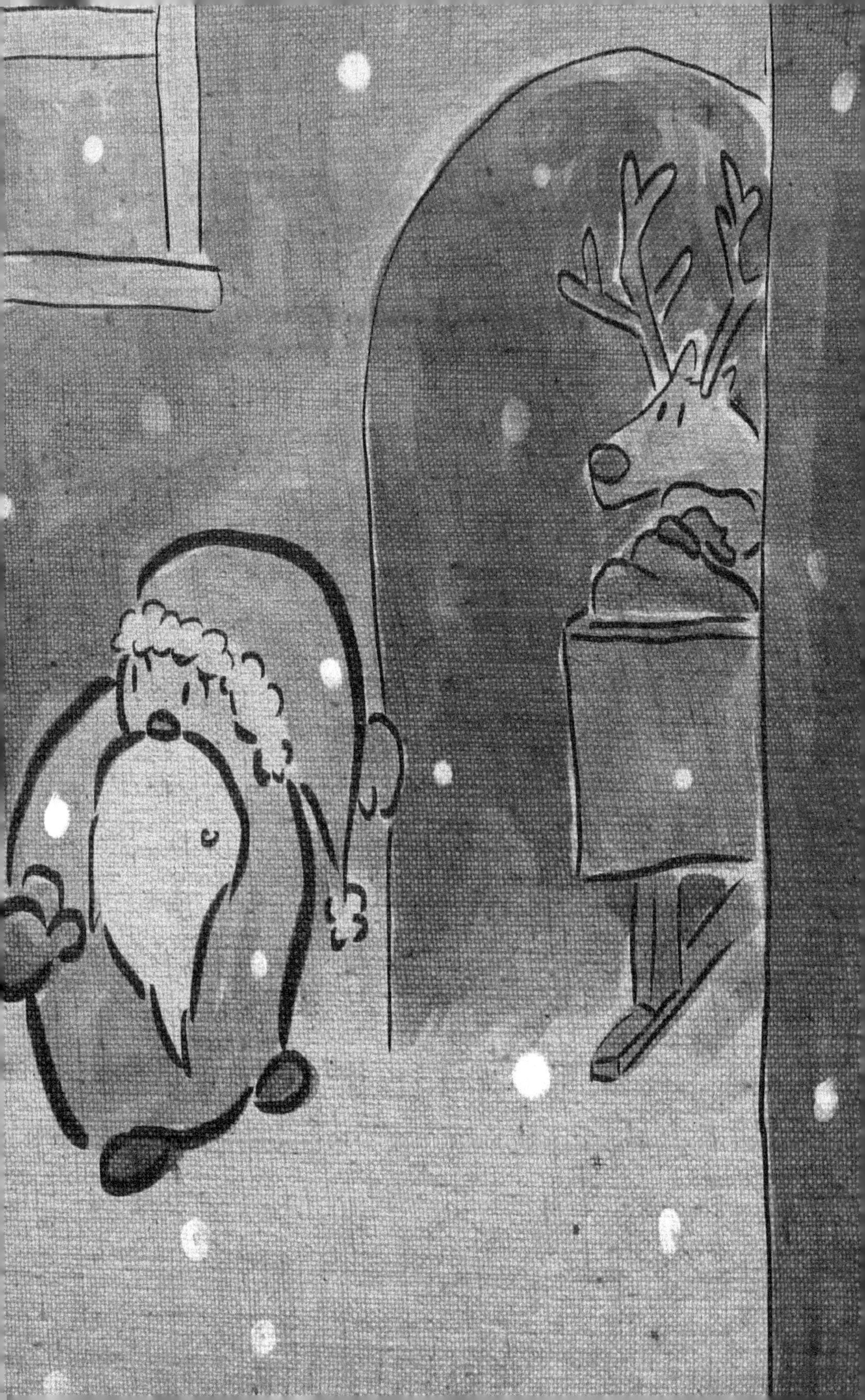

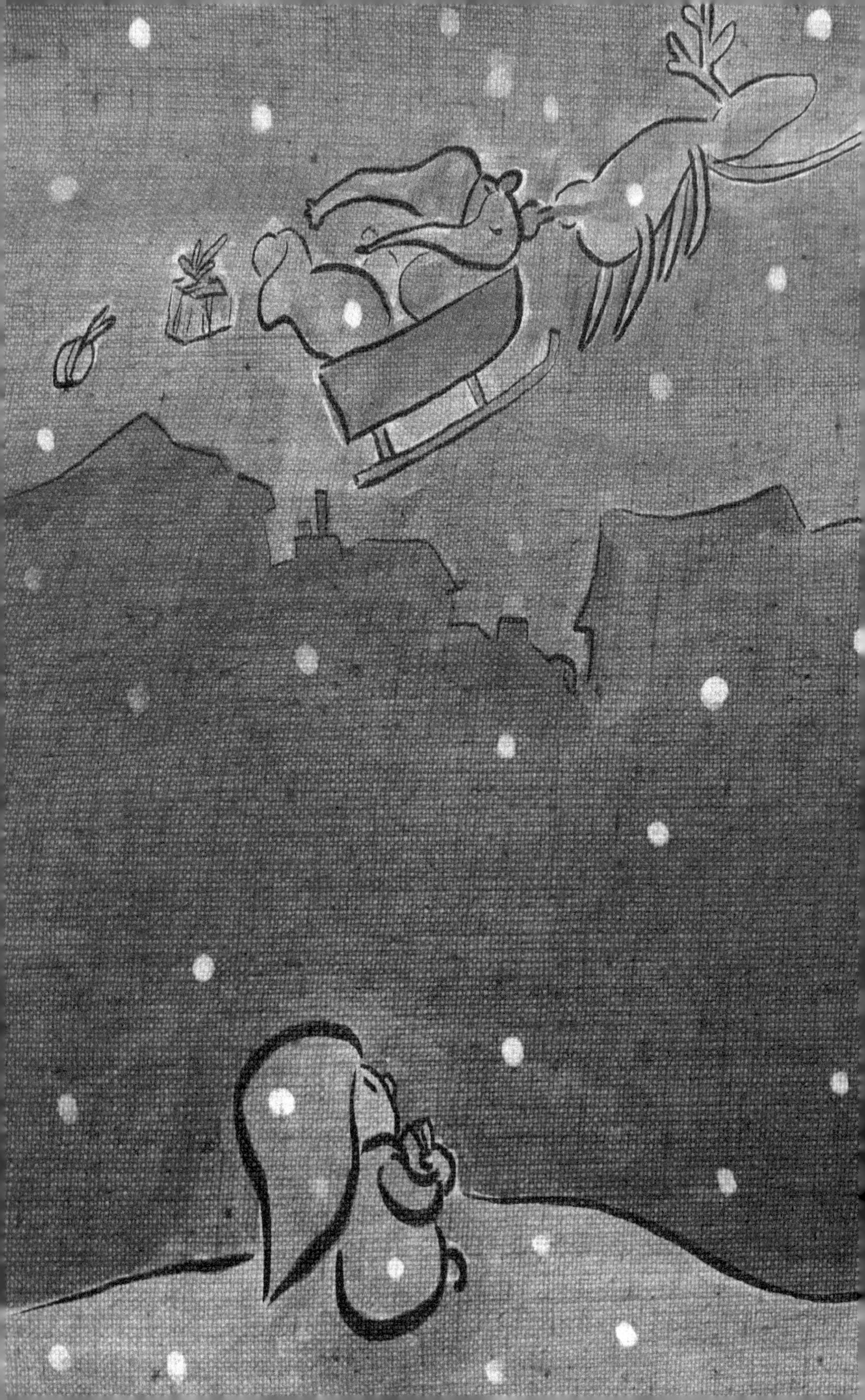

Lightning Source UK Ltd.
Milton Keynes UK
UKHW022331170119
335721UK00009B/174/P

9 780368 033711